Wait! Wait!

The illustrations were created using acrylic and oil pencils.

Translated from the Japanese by Yuki Kaneko

www.enchantedlion.com

First American Edition published in 2013 by Enchanted Lion Books, 20 Jay Street, Studio M-18, Brooklyn, NY 11201
Translation copyright © 2013 by Enchanted Lion Books
Text copyright © 2002 by Hatsue Nakawaki
Illustration copyright © 2002 by Komako Sakai
Originally published by Fukuinkan Shoten Publishers, Inc., Tokyo, Japan under the title *Korya Mate Mate*.
English rights arranged with Fukuinkan Shoten Publishers, Inc., Tokyo, Japan.
All rights reserved under International and Pan-American Copyright Conventions
A CIP record is on file with the Library of Congress
ISBN: 978-1-59270-138-4
Printed in March 2013 in China by South China Printing Co. Ltd.

Wait! Wait!

By Hatsue Nakawaki
Illustrated by Komako Sakai

ENCHANTED LION BOOKS
NEW YORK

Wait! Wait!

Fluttering up in the air.

Wait! Wait!

Wiggling out of sight.

Wait! Wait!

Flapping wings
and flying away.

Wait! Wait!

Meow. Meow. Meow.

Wait! Wait!

Here we go!